J. S. BACH

MW01285431

SEVEN TOCCATAS
BWV 910–916
FOR THE KEYBOARD

EDITED BY HANS BISCHOFF

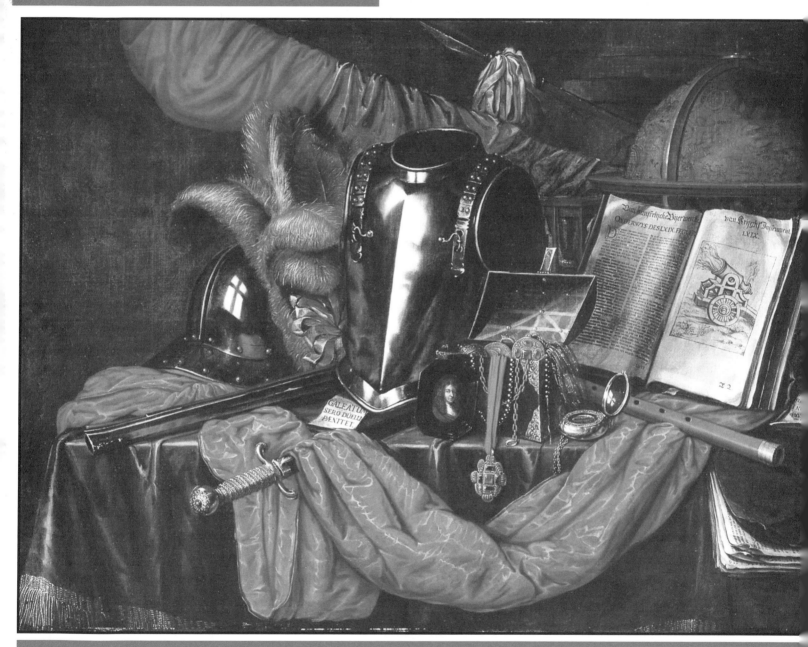

AN ALFRED MASTERWORK EDITION

Copyright © 2015 by Alfred Music
All rights reserved.   Printed in USA.
ISBN-10: 1-4706-2282-3
ISBN-13: 978-1-4706-2282-4

Cover art: Vanitas Still Life *(1669)*
By Edwaert Collier (Dutch, ca. 1642–1708)
Oil on canvas

JOHANN SEBASTIAN BACH

Contents

About Hans Bischoff and This Edition 2

Introductory Notes 2

Table of Embellishments 3

SEVEN TOCCATAS

Toccata in D Major, BWV 912 4

Toccata in D Minor, BWV 913 18

Toccata in C Minor, BWV 911 34

Toccata in F-sharp Minor, BWV 910 50

Toccata in G Minor, BWV 915 66

Toccata in G Major, BWV 916 80

Toccata in E Minor, BWV 914 90

ABOUT HANS BISCHOFF AND THIS EDITION

Hans Bischoff (1852–1889) was a German concert pianist, chamber musician, and music educator. He studied piano with Theodor Kullak (1818–1882) and later taught piano performance and music theory at Kullak's school, Neue Akademie der Tonkunst, in Berlin. Bischoff became a well-regarded music editor, respected for his thorough research, attention to detail, and careful consideration of source materials. His critical editions for the Steingräber publishing house include seven volumes of the keyboard works by J. S. Bach and 11 volumes of the keyboard works by Robert Schumann, as well as editions of works by Clementi, Handel, Mozart, Schubert, and Weber.

Bischoff's footnotes and prefatory commentary have been preserved in this edition, as well as his editorial markings—suggested dynamics, metronome marks, fingering, articulations, and pedaling. Measure numbers and BWV numbers have been added. Square brackets have been used to indicate suspected missing elements from earlier Bischoff editions.

INTRODUCTORY NOTES

Toccata in D Major – Our text is based on two old manuscripts in the possession of Dr. W. Rust, of Leipzig. One of these is signed: *F. W. Rust*; the other is from the estate of Sarah Levy, a pupil of [Carl] Philipp Emanuel Bach. We have also compared the available printed editions, as well as two manuscripts from the State Library in Berlin.

Toccata in G Minor – I have, unfortunately, been unable to secure any manuscript material for the publication of this work. I have been informed by Mr. Roitzch that the work was edited on the basis of a copy belonging to Mr. F. Hauser. This was later compared by Mr. Griepenkerl with another manuscript stemming from Forkel's legacy. I have been able to secure no information regarding the present whereabouts of these sources.

Both of the Peters publications agree on all important points and give rise to no special problems. There are two problematical places in the first *Allegro* in B-flat which have occurred to me; however, I do not consider them important enough to warrant altering the text as it appears in Ed. Peters.

Toccata in G Major – We have compared the following manuscripts: *A* (P. 279) and *B* (P. 281) from the Royal Library in Berlin; *C*, a manuscript from the Krebs collection belonging to Mr. Roitzsch; *D* (P. 289) from the Royal Library in Berlin; finally, the edition printed by Peters. The deviations in the various sources are more numerous than they are important. In the main, the text is clearly legible. Certain details can be left to the discretion of the performer. The manuscripts contain a mass of obviously unauthentic ornamentation which is quite unworthy of mention. Moreover, the manuscripts are frequently in conspicuous agreement in the matter of errors in script. We hope that our footnotes will prove that we have made no arbitrary emendations. We should like to add that we did not see the Gerber manuscript until after the engraving for this volume had been completed.

Toccata in E Minor – Three copies of this toccata are preserved in the Berlin Royal Library. They are numbered P. 213, 275 and 295. We refer to them as *A*, *B*, and *C* respectively. The first of these contains two fugues of which the second constitutes the finale of the *Toccata in E-minor*. The opening section of this composition was missing in this manuscript; but a copy of it, written in a

Seven Toccatas, BWV 910–916

Edited by Hans Bischoff

different handwriting, was added and bound together with the rest of the manuscript. The differences in text among the various manuscripts as well as the deviations between them and the edition prepared by Griepenkerl for Ed. Peters are worthy of note. The *Adagio* is missing in *B* and *C*; there are also other elements indicating a probable common source for both mauscripts. This *Adagio* may have been composed later as an addition to this *Toccata*. We consider it unauthentic for this reason alone. It is related to other middle movements in Bach's *Toccatas* both in inspiration and in mood. The variants are relatively unimportant up to the ending of the *Adagio*. The final fugue contains many more deviations in text. In *A* practically all the variants under consideration have been added in a strange handwriting. The character of these leaves no doubt in my mind that Bach himself had made a number of copies of this work in which he incorporated these changes—some of which were planned corrections, others merely incidental and cursory changes. In view of the lack of an absolutely authoritative source, it is impossible to determine the question of absolute authenticity; however, it is possible for the editor to present an authentic, correct text—making special note of all important variants. Moreover, errors in script are sometimes presented as actual variants in *A*. We have to present most of the ornaments in smaller type—in view of the fact that their authenticity is not absolutely established. P.S. I have compared the Gerber copy after the type-setting had been completed.

All the ornaments indicated in this text are authentic, but only those printed in large type represent Bach's irrevocable intentions. The latter must be played. On the other hand, the execution of the ornaments in smaller type may be left to the discretion of the performer.

TABLE OF EMBELLISHMENTS

For the uninitiated performer the following indications will suffice—in reference to this volume.

1)   Grace notes, like all other embellishments, enter ON the beat—not before it. Unless indicated otherwise, they should be executed quickly.

2)   The trill (*tr* or ⁓⁓) generally begins on the auxiliary note. There is usually an after-beat, unless this is replaced by one or more indicated notes. The after-beat is unnecessary before a descending second. The symbol for the trill with an upbeat is ⁓⁓⌣ or ⁓⁓⌣ . The trill starting on the lower note ⁓⁓ and the one starting on the upper note ⁓⁓ usually both end with an after-beat. The following symbols may also be used to indicate the same: ⌣⁓ and ⁓⁓ . The short trill ⁓ is usually tied to the upper second preceding. Its symbol frequently takes the place of ⁓⁓ and *tr* .

3)   The mordent or often takes the tone a minor second lower as the auxiliary note, although the neighboring note is sometimes a major second lower.

4)   The turn ∾ placed over a note is executed , placed between two notes it is played . In dotted rhythm, the turn proper ends on the dot .

5)   The slurred note ⁓ is played .

6)   Other embellishments are explained in the annotations.

Dr. Hans Bischoff

SEVEN TOCCATAS

Toccata in D Major

(Fantasie and Fugue)

Johann Sebastian Bach (1685–1750)
BWV 912

1) There is a figurative deviation in the first five measures—in Griepenkerl.

2) This tempo indication is taken from the manuscripts.

1) This as well as the ensuing analogous "chords of the sixth" appear in Ed. Peters with a doubled root.

2) One finds distortions of the figuration in the manuscripts. The three ensuing measures are missing in Griepenkerl.

1) The F. W. Rust manuscript has the following inferior reading:

2) One sometimes finds D-natural in place of D-sharp.

1) The **p** indication appears in the manuscripts.

2) The **f** indication appears in the manuscripts.

3) This tempo indication is taken from the manuscripts.

1) Here and in several analogous places the Peters edition has a chord on the strong beat. To the best of my knowledge this is not in accordance with tradition.

2) From this point on one also finds D-sharp in place of D-natural.

3) According to Griepenkerl: *Allegro moderato* (♩ = 88). The manuscripts generally do not indicate any change of pace. The editor recommends for this section a mood of simple expressiveness combined with a measured gravity of movement as well as extremely legato execution.

4) The tie is missing at this point as well as in analogous places subsequently.

1) The editor believes that the E-sharp is correct. The traditional note is E-natural.

1) Occasionally one finds E-sharp instead of E-natural on the fourth eighth. In that case the E-natural enters on the fifth eighth.
2) The words "con discrezione" as well as the little slurs are taken from the manuscripts.
3) A-sharp instead of A-natural according to F. W. Rust.

1) This is an inverted mordent.

2) "Presto" appears in the manuscripts.

3) D instead of E in Peters.

1) The countersubject sometimes has the perfect fourth, sometimes the augmented fourth. In places where the authorities disagree I have followed the Rust manuscript.

1) This middle voice appears in Peters. I have never found it in any of the manuscripts.

2) Elsewhere one finds D instead of E.

1) The manuscripts have F-sharp instead of F-natural. Ed. Peters has the F-natural.

Toccata in D Minor

BWV 913

1) Both Chrysander and Reinecke have the following:

1) Execute the slide as follows:

FUGA

Presto ($\textbf{\textit{♩}}$ = 96)

1) The following is a plausible execution of the theme:

The remainder should be played strictly legato.

1) Some of the manuscripts substitute an A for the C.

1) The ensuing passage requires a moderate use of the pedal.

FUGA
(♩ = 104)

1) Elsewhere one finds B-natural instead of B-flat. In general, there appear considerable discrepancies apropos the modulatory character of the sequences.

1) Griepenkerl and Peters both have: [music example]

1) Others substitute B-natural for the B-flat—similarly in the next measure.

Toccata in C Minor

1) A number of editions have F-sharp instead of F.

2) Other editions have B-flat instead of C.

1) The F is a correction based on Peters. The F-sharp appearing in the Bach-Gesellschaft edition is very unmelodic.

1) Other editions contain the following weakened harmony: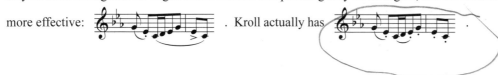

2) This is an A-flat in several manuscripts.

3) The fugue should be accented in a very lively manner. The **p** appearing in our text at the reentrance of the first motive may be used throughout the fugue if one wishes. The phrasing may be all legato; but the following is better and much

more effective: . Kroll actually has .

1) In view of the fact that this passage (as well as analogous passages) has been handed down to us in extremely contradictory versions, and since it seems definitely improbable that Bach desired any heterogeneity in these passages, the editor felt that the second beat should remain in the key, whereas the second sixteenth note in the third beat should be chromatically raised. This conclusion was reached after perusing all the available texts.

2) This is a short trill without an after-beat:

3) The A-natural is preferred by the editor in place of A-flat as a result of comparison with analogous passages.

1) This is a deviation in the rhythmic structure of the theme to make it more easily playable.

2) Kroll has A-flat instead of A-natural.

3) Peters has

1) E-natural instead of E-flat in the Bach-Gesellschaft edition.

2) A-natural instead of A-flat and E-natural instead of E-flat in the Bach-Gesellschaft edition.

1) A-flat instead of A-natural in other editions.

2) One finds the following in some manuscripts:

3) The Bach-Gesellschaft edition always has A-flat instead of A-natural. One rarely finds complete unanimity in the manuscripts in the structure of the descending minor scale.

4) The appoggiatura is a long note:

5) B-flat instead of B-natural in other editions.

1) The probable execution should be

1) Other editions have F instead of E-flat. This is erroneous.

1) Other editions have A-natural instead of A-flat here and in the next quarter.

Toccata in F-sharp Minor

Lento e molto espressivo (♩ = 60)

1) The first motive should always be projected singingly.

2) Edition Peters has a long trill here and in analogous places.

3) The appoggiatura is a long note.

1) Apropos the poor rhythmic division, see Rust's prefaces to the 22nd and 23rd annual publications of the Bach Gesellschaft.

2) The suspension is a long note. It is best to delay the *Presto* till the entrance of the eighth notes. The *staccato* indication is traditional. The entire fugue should be accentuated in a spirited manner.

3) The variant in Peters (see Vol. 4, no. 4) is preferable to our text. However, it is not sufficiently authenticated.

1) A-sharp more often than A-natural in a number of manuscripts as well as in Peters.

2) The pattern  appears in Peters throughout three and a half measures.

1) The Bach-Gesellschaft edition erroneously has C-sharp instead of D.

2) This is the editor's own version. Other texts contain

1) The A-sharp appearing in the editions with which I am familiar as well as in the manuscripts is extremely improbable.

2) The Bach-Gesellschaft erroneously has F-sharp.

3) One frequently finds F-double-sharp instead of F-sharp. This is erroneous.

1) In the manuscripts one finds D-sharp instead of D.

1) Ed. Peters inserts the following measure at this point:  I have never seen it elsewhere.

2) The tempo here is quieter, approximately ♩ = 80.

1) The editor surmises the B-sharp to be correct. Other editions have B-natural.

2) The B is in conformity with analogous places. Other editions contain B-sharp.

1) Peters has A-sharp instead of A-natural.

1) ♮ in Peters.

Toccata in G Minor

BWV 915

NB. 1 The suspension should be played as a half note.

NB. 2 I think that an actual mordent was really intended here in place of the inverted mordent.

1) The absence of the flat sign in comparison with the other two analogous places (indicated by the *1)* sign [at measures 8 and 22]) is conspicuous. This is probably an error in script.

NB. 1 The suspension should be played as a quarter note.

NB. 2 The suspension should be played as a half note.

1) See page 67, note 1.

1) See page 67, note 1.

2) I have two suggestions to offer in reference to this measure. First, the second eighth note in the soprano should really be G instead of B-flat. Secondly, the final eighth beat in the measure should contain the chord consisting of D, F-sharp, and A—analogously to similar passages and to the chord on the fourth eighth of the ensuing measure.

FUGA
Allegro ma non troppo (♩ = 116)

NB. In view of the continuous triplet figuration in the counterpoint, the theme is to be played as if it were written in $\frac{12}{8}$ time, consisting of quarter notes and eighth notes—thus: ‖ 𝄾· 𝄾 ♪♩ ♪♩ ♪ ‖ . In other words, the sixteenth note coincides with the last eighth note in the triplet.

NB. The notes in parentheses are not to be played.

Toccata in G Major

BWV 916

1) In Peters and in *C* the rest is replaced by an eighth note on D.

2) In Peters the rest is replaced by an eighth note on A.

NB. 1 The manuscript *C* contains a large number of spurious ornaments which we do not reprint. The same manuscript contains ties at the places indicated by the sign ⊕.

NB. 2 The mordents appear in the Peters edition.

1) Here again the eighth note on A is added in the Peters edition.

2) In Peters the repeated high notes are frequently tied.

3) In *A* and *B* this D appears on the fourth beat.

4) Presumably through an error in script, the high voice in *A* appears as follows:

5) The B and E are missing in *A, B, C,* and *D*.

6) C instead of B in *B* through an error in script.

7) Ed. Peters substitutes C for this B. The latter is substantiated by *A, B, C,* and *D*.

8) An E is added to this chord in Ed. Peters and *C*.

1) An E is added to this chord in Ed. Peters and *C*.

1) This E is replaced by G in *A*.

1) A instead of F-sharp in *A*.

2) This C-sharp is missing in *A, B, C,* and *D*; it does appear in Ed. Peters.

3) According to Ed. Peters: [♩ notation]. The G-sharp also appears in Gerber.

4) The natural sign is missing in *C* and *D*.

NB. In the *Adagio* as well as the ensuing fugue the *A* manuscript contains a large number or ornaments, many of which are obviously spurious. Moreover, they are not authenticated in *B, C, D,* or Ed. Peters. A tie is occasionally omitted in *A* and *B*.

1) In a number of instances one finds G instead of A.

2) F-sharp instead of E in Ed. Peters—similarly in Gerber.

3) This tie appears only in *A*.

4) D instead of F-sharp—an error in script both in *B* and *C*.

1) D instead of F-sharp—an error in script found in *A, B,* and *C.*

2) There is a sharp at this point in *A* and *C*; in *B* the sharp has been erased.

3) Also at this point *A* and *C* contain the erroneous C-sharp instead of C-natural. In *D* and in Gerber one finds the succession C-sharp, D-sharp; this is quite plausible.

4) D-sharp instead of D according to Ed. Peters.

5) The sharp is missing in *A* and *C. B* contains a B-natural in place of C-sharp.

1) *B* originally contained  ; this was subsequently corrected to  . The E and D are also found in *C*.

2) The common error in script appearing in *A, B,* and *C*, wherein the F-sharp is replaced by a D, has been justifiably corrected in Ed. Peters.

3) D-sharp in place of D according to *C, D,* and Ed. Peters.

4) There is a sharp before the C in Ed. Peters.

1) The natural sign has been omitted in *A* and *B*.

1) D instead of E in *B*. Moreover, the final sixteenth note in the previous measure is a D in the *D* manuscript. Gerber has .

2) This version taken from the *D* manuscript seems to us to be more plausible than any of the other various versions appearing in the different manuscripts.

3) This F-sharp is missing in *A* and *B*.

4) The D replacing the B at this point is probably an error in script in some of the sources.

5) Some of the ties appear in *C*, others appear in Ed. Peters.

6) G-natural instead of A in Ed. Peters, i.e., analogously to the next measure; similarly in Gerber.

7) In *A* the bass is  . In *B* the entire first half of this measure is missing.

Toccata in E Minor

BWV 914

1) A-sharp instead of A in Ed. Peters.

2) G instead of G-sharp in various sources.

Un poco Allegro (♩ = 76)

molto legato

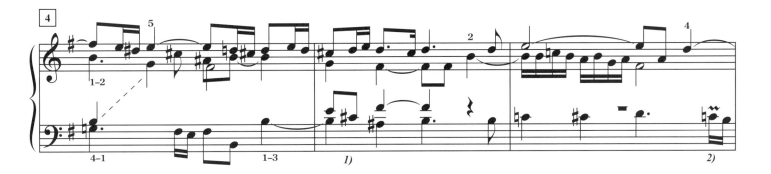

1) This C-sharp is missing in two of the manuscripts.

2) C-sharp according to Ed. Peters. This is highly questionable.

1) In Ed. Peters there is first D-sharp then D-natural.

1) The C is missing in *A*.

2) In this one instance *A* contains C-sharp instead of C.

3) The G-sharp is missing in *A*. The ties are not always carefully indicated in this manuscript.

4) Variant in *A*:   .   Gerber has   .

1) Variant from *A*. The natural sign before the D is not actually written in; but it should definitely be added in view of the general character of this variant.

In this manuscript the transition to G major is indicated by this scale. Gerber seems to be in agreement with this ms.

2) The natural sign before the F is omitted in *A*.

3) D-sharp instead of B in *A*.

4) In *A* one finds F-sharp and A instead of A and C. Similarly in Gerber.

FUGA (a 3 voci)

Allegro ($\quad$ = 108)

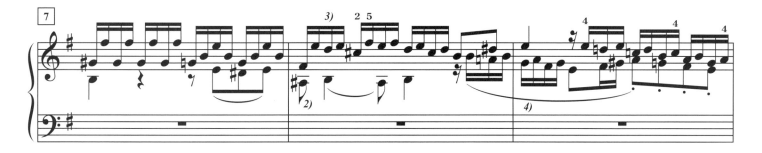

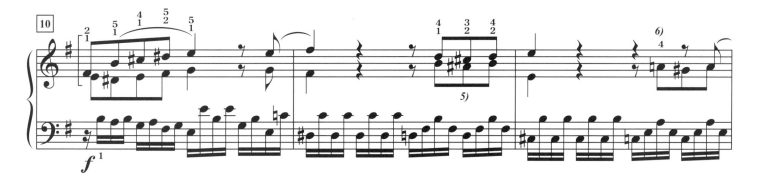

1) According to *A*: . This is highly questionable.

2) Variant: .

3) D-sharp replaced the D at this point in *A*. In *B, C,* and Gerber, the D-sharp enters on the third quarter.

4) Variant: G-sharp instead of G.

5) Variant: A instead of A-sharp.

6) Variant: .

1) Variant:

2) Variant:

3) Variant:

4) Variant in the middle voice:

5) Variant: B instead of A.

6) Variant:

7) Variant:

1) Variant:

2) In Ed. Peters there appears the following middle voice, which is not to be found in the variants contained in *A* and is also missing in *B* and *C*: . I have indicated other deviations by means of accidentals in parentheses.

3) Variant: F-sharp instead of E.

4) Variant:

5) Variant:

6) Variant: G instead of A.

7) Variant: B instead of A.

8) Variant:

9) Variant:

1) Variant: [music notation]

2) The B and E are missing from the text in *A*.

3) Originally one quarter instead of two eighths in *A*.

4) Variant: [music notation]

5) Variant: [music notation]

6) Variant: A and E instead of two F-sharps an octave apart.

1) Variant:

2) Variant: F-sharp instead of B.

3) Variant:

4) Variant:

5) Variant:

6) According to some sources D-sharp instead of E
   from the fourth eighth on.